THE DREAM OF A RIDICULOUS MAN
(1877)

THE DREAM OF A RIDICULOUS MAN (1877)

FYODOR DOSTOEVSKY

Translated
by
Constance Garnett

GYAN

Published by

Gyan Publishing House
5, Ansari Road
Daryaganj, New Delhi-110002
Phone: 011-47034999, 9811692060
E-mail: books@gyanbooks.com

Distribution Network
gyanbooks.com
India, USA, Canada, UK, Australia, France

ISBN: 978-93-6208-264-0 (HB)
First Published, 2024

Printed at: Gyan Press, Delhi.

THE DREAM OF A RIDICULOUS MAN (1877)
Author: Fyodor Dostoevsky

CONTENTS

CHAPTER - I

I am a ridiculous person. Now they call me a madman. That would be a promotion if it were not that I remain as ridiculous in their eyes as before. But now I do not resent it, they are all dear to me now, even when they laugh at me - and, indeed, it is just then that they are particularly dear to me. I could join in their laughter—not exactly at myself, but through affection for them, if I did not feel so sad as I look at them. Sad because they do not know the truth and I do know it. Oh, how hard it is to be the only one who knows the truth! But they won't understand that. No, they won't understand it.

In old days I used to be miserable at seeming ridiculous. Not seeming, but being. I have always been ridiculous, and I have known it, perhaps, from the hour I was born. Perhaps from the time I was seven years old I knew I was ridiculous. Afterwards I went to school, studied at the university, and, do you know, the more I learned, the more thoroughly I understood that I was ridiculous. So that it seemed in the end as though all the sciences I studied at the university existed only to prove and make evident to me as I went more deeply into them that I was ridiculous. It was the same with life as it was with science. With every year the same consciousness of the ridiculous figure I cut in every relation grew and strengthened. Everyone always laughed at me. But not one of them knew or guessed that if there were one man on earth who knew better than anybody else that I was absurd, it was myself, and what I resented most of all was that they did not know that. But that was my own fault; I was so proud that nothing would have ever induced me to tell it to anyone. This pride grew in me with the years; and if it had happened that I allowed myself to confess to anyone that I was ridiculous, I believe that I should have blown out my brains the same evening. Oh, how I suffered in my early youth from the fear that I might give way and confess it to my schoolfellows. But since I grew to manhood, I have for some unknown reason become calmer, though I realised my awful characteristic more fully every year. I say 'unknown', for to this day I cannot tell why it was. Perhaps it was owing to the terrible misery that was growing in my soul through something which was of more consequence than anything else about me: that something was the conviction that had come upon me that nothing in the world mattered. I had long had an inkling of it, but the full realisation came last year almost suddenly. I suddenly felt that it was all the same to me whether the world existed or whether there had never been anything at all: I began to feel with all my being that there was nothing existing. At first I fancied that many things had existed in the past, but afterwards I guessed that there never had been anything in the past either, but that it had only seemed so for some reason. Little by little I guessed that there would be nothing in the future either. Then I left off being angry with people and almost ceased to notice them. Indeed this showed itself even in the pettiest trifles: I used, for instance, to knock against people in the street. And not so much from being lost in thought: what had I to think about? I had almost given up thinking by that time; nothing mattered to me. If at least I had solved my problems! Oh, I had not settled one of them, and how many there were! But I gave up caring about anything, and all the problems disappeared.

And it was after that that I found out the truth. I learnt the truth last November—on the third of November, to be precise—and I remember every instant since. It was a gloomy evening, one of the gloomiest possible evenings. I was going home at about eleven o'clock, and I remember that I thought that the evening could not be gloomier. Even physically. Rain had been falling all day, and it had been a cold, gloomy, almost menacing rain, with, I remember, an unmistakable spite against mankind. Suddenly between ten and eleven it had stopped, and was followed by a horrible dampness, colder and damper than the rain, and a sort of steam was rising from everything, from every stone in the street, and from every by-lane if one looked down it as far as one could. A thought suddenly occurred to me, that if all the street lamps had been put out it would have been less cheerless, that the gas made one's heart sadder because it lighted it all up. I had had scarcely any dinner that day, and had been spending the evening with an engineer, and two other friends had been there also. I sat silent—I fancy I bored them. They talked of something rousing and suddenly they got excited over it. But they did not really care, I could see that, and only made a show of being excited. I suddenly said as much to them. "My friends," I said, "you really do not care one way or the other." They were not offended, but they laughed at me. That was because I spoke without any not of reproach, simply because it did not matter to me. They saw it did not, and it amused them.

As I was thinking about the gas lamps in the street I looked up at the sky. The sky was horribly dark, but one could distinctly see tattered clouds, and between them fathomless black patches. Suddenly I noticed in one of these patches a star, and began watching it intently. That was because that star had given me an idea: I decided to kill myself that night. I had firmly determined to do so two months before, and poor as I was, I bought a splendid revolver that very day, and loaded it. But two months had passed and it was still lying in my drawer; I was so utterly indifferent that I wanted to seize a moment when I would not be so indifferent—why, I don't know. And so for two months every night that I came home I thought I would shoot myself. I kept waiting for the right moment. And so now this star gave me a thought. I made up my mind that it should certainly be that night. And why the star gave me the thought I don't know.

And just as I was looking at the sky, this little girl took me by the elbow. The street was empty, and there was scarcely anyone to be seen. A cabman was sleeping in the distance in his cab. It was a child of eight with a kerchief on her head, wearing nothing but a wretched little dress all soaked with rain, but I noticed her wet broken shoes and I recall them now. They caught my eye particularly. She suddenly pulled me by the elbow and called me. She was not weeping, but was spasmodically crying out some words which could not utter properly, because she was shivering and shuddering all over. She was in terror about something, and kept crying, "Mammy, mammy!" I turned facing her, I did not say a word and went on; but she ran, pulling at me, and there was that note in her voice which in frightened children means despair. I know that sound. Though she did not articulate the words, I understood that her mother was dying, or that something of the sort was happening to them, and that she had run out to call someone, to find something to help her mother. I did not go with her; on the contrary, I had an impulse to drive her away. I told her first to go to a policeman. But clasping her hands, she ran beside me sobbing and gasping, and would not leave me. Then I stamped my foot and shouted at her. She called out "Sir! sir! . . ." but suddenly abandoned me and rushed headlong across the road. Some other passerby appeared there, and she evidently flew from me to him.

I mounted up to my fifth storey. I have a room in a flat where there are other lodgers. My room is small and poor, with a garret window in the shape of a semicircle. I have a sofa covered with American leather, a table with books on it, two chairs and a comfortable arm-chair, as old as old can be, but of the good old-fashioned shape. I sat down, lighted the candle, and began thinking.

In the room next to mine, through the partition wall, a perfect Bedlam was going on. It had been going on for the last three days. A retired captain lived there, and he had half a dozen visitors, gentlemen of doubtful reputation, drinking *vodka* and playing stoss with old cards. The night before there had been a fight, and I know that two of them had been for a long time engaged in dragging each other about by the hair. The landlady wanted to complain, but she was in abject terror of the captain. There was only one other lodger in the flat, a thin little regimental lady, on a visit to Petersburg, with three little children who had been taken ill since they came into the lodgings. Both she and her children were in mortal fear of the captain, and lay trembling and crossing themselves all night, and the youngest child had a sort of fit from fright. That captain, I know for a fact, sometimes stops people in the Nevsky Prospect and begs. They won't take him into the service, but strange to say (that's why I am telling this), all this month that the captain has been here his behavior has caused me no annoyance. I have, of course, tried to avoid his acquaintance from the very beginning, and he, too, was bored with me from the first; but I never care how much they shout the other side of the partition nor how many of them there are in there: I sit up all night and forget them so completely that I do not even hear them. I stay awake till daybreak, and have been going on like that for the last year. I sit up all night in my arm-chair at the table, doing nothing. I only read by day. I sit—don't even think; ideas of a sort wander through my mind and I let them come and go as they will. A whole candle is burnt every night. I sat down quietly at the table, took out the revolver and put it down before me. When I had put it down I asked myself, I remember, "Is that so?" and answered with complete conviction, "It is." That is, I shall shoot myself. I knew that I should shoot myself that night for certain, but how much longer I should go on sitting at the table I did not know. And no doubt I should have shot myself if it had not been for that little girl.

CHAPTER - II

You see, though nothing mattered to me, I could feel pain, for instance. If anyone had stuck me it would have hurt me. It was the same morally: if anything very pathetic happened, I should have felt pity just as I used to do in old days when there were things in life that did matter to me. I had felt pity that evening. I should have certainly helped a child. Why, then, had I not helped the little girl? Because of an idea that occurred to me at the time: when she was calling and pulling at me, a question suddenly arose before me and I could not settle it. The question was an idle one, but I was vexed. I was vexed at the reflection that if I were going to make an end of myself that night, nothing in life ought to have mattered to me. Why was it that all at once I did not feel a strange pang, quite incongruous in my position. Really I do not know better how to convey my fleeting sensation at the moment, but the sensation persisted at home when I was sitting at the table, and I was very much irritated as I had not been for a long time past. One reflection followed another. I saw clearly that so long as I was still a human being and not nothingness, I was alive and so could suffer, be angry and feel shame at my actions. So be it. But if I am going to kill myself, in two hours, say, what is the little girl to me and what have I to do with shame or with anything else in the world? I shall turn into nothing, absolutely nothing. And can it really be true that the consciousness that I shall completely cease to exist immediately and so everything else will cease to exist, does not in the least affect my feeling of pity for the child nor the feeling of shame after a contemptible action? I stamped and shouted at the unhappy child as though to say—not only I feel no pity, but even if I behave inhumanly and contemptibly, I am free to, for in another two hours everything will be extinguished. Do you believe that that was why I shouted that? I am almost convinced of it now. It seemed clear to me that life and the world somehow depended upon me now. I may almost say that the world now seemed created for me alone: if I shot myself the world would cease to be at least for me. I say nothing of its being likely that nothing will exist for anyone when I am gone, and that as soon as my consciousness is extinguished the whole world will vanish too and become void like a phantom, as a mere appurtenance of my consciousness, for possibly all this world and all these people are only me myself.

I remember that as I sat and reflected, I turned all these new questions that swarmed one after another quite the other way, and thought of something quite new. For instance, a strange reflection suddenly occurred to me, that if I had lived before on the moon or on Mars and there had committed the most disgraceful and dishonourable action and had there been put to such shame and ignominy as one can only conceive and realise in dreams, in nightmares, and if, finding myself afterwards on earth, I were able to retain the memory of what I had done on the other planet and at the same time knew that I should never, under any circumstances, return there, then looking from the earth to the moon—should I care or not? Should I feel shame for that action or not? These were idle and superfluous questions for the revolver was already lying before me, and I knew in every fibre of my being that it would happen for certain, but they excited me and I raged. I could not die now without having first settled something. In short, the child had saved me, for I put off my pistol shot for the sake of these questions. Meanwhile the clamour had begun to subside in the captain's room: they had finished their game, were settling down to sleep, and meanwhile were grumbling and languidly winding up their quarrels. At that point, I suddenly fell asleep in my chair at the table—a thing which had never happened to me before. I dropped asleep quite unawares.

Dreams, as we all know, are very queer things: some parts are presented with appalling vividness, with details worked up with the elaborate finish of jewellery, while others one gallops through, as it were, without noticing them at all, as, for instance, through space and time. Dreams seem to be spurred on not by reason but by desire, not by the head but by the heart, and yet what complicated tricks my reason has played sometimes in dreams, what utterly incomprehensible things happen to it! My brother died five years ago, for instance. I sometimes dream of him; he takes part in my affairs, we are very much interested, and yet all through my dream I quite know and remember that my brother is dead and buried. How is it that I am not surprised that, though he is dead, he is here beside me and working with me? Why is it that my reason fully accepts it? But enough. I will begin about my dream. Yes, I dreamed a dream, my dream of the third of November. They tease me now, telling me it was only a dream. But does it matter whether it was a dream or reality, if the dream made known to me the truth? If once one has recognized the truth and seen it, you know that it is the truth and that there is no other and there cannot be, whether you are asleep or awake. Let it be a dream, so be it, but that real life of which you make so much I had meant to extinguish by suicide, and my dream, my dream—oh, it revealed to me a different life, renewed, grand and full of power!

Listen.

CHAPTER - III

I have mentioned that I dropped asleep unawares and even seemed to be still reflecting on the same subjects. I suddenly dreamt that I picked up the revolver and aimed it straight at my heart—my heart, and not my head; and I had determined beforehand to fire at my head, at my right temple. After aiming at my chest I waited a second or two, and suddenly my candle, my table, and the wall in front of me began moving and heaving. I made haste to pull the trigger.

In dreams you sometimes fall from a height, or are stabbed, or beaten, but you never feel pain unless, perhaps, you really bruise yourself against the bedstead, then you feel pain and almost always wake up from it. It was the same in my dream. I did not feel any pain, but it seemed as though with my shot everything within me was shaken and everything was suddenly dimmed, and it grew horribly black around me. I seemed to be blinded, and it benumbed, and I was lying on something hard, stretched on my back; I saw nothing, and could not make the slightest movement. People were walking and shouting around me, the captain bawled, the landlady shrieked—and suddenly another break and I was being carried in a closed coffin. And I felt how the coffin was shaking and reflected upon it, and for the first time the idea struck me that I was dead, utterly dead, I knew it and had no doubt of it, I could neither see nor move and yet I was feeling and reflecting. But I was soon reconciled to the position, and as one usually does in a dream, accepted the facts without disputing them.

And now I was buried in the earth. They all went away, I was left alone, utterly alone. I did not move. Whenever before I had imagined being buried the one sensation I associated with the grave was that of damp and cold. So now I felt that I was very cold, especially the tips of my toes, but I felt nothing else.

I lay still, strange to say I expected nothing, accepting without dispute that a dead man had nothing to expect. But it was damp. I don't know how long a time passed—whether an hour or several days, or many days. But all at once a drop of water fell on my closed left eye, making its way through the coffin lid; it was followed a minute later by a second, then a minute later by a third—and so on, regularly every minute. There was a sudden glow of profound indignation in my heart, and I suddenly felt in it a pang of physical pain. "That's my wound," I thought; "that's the bullet . . ." And drop after drop every minute kept falling on my closed eyelid. And all at once, not with my voice, but with my entire being, I called upon the power that was responsible for all that was happening to me:

"Whoever you may be, if you exist, and if anything more rational that what is happening here is possible, suffer it to be here now. But if you are revenging yourself upon me for my senseless suicide by the hideousness and absurdity of this subsequent existence, then let me tell you that no torture could ever equal the contempt which I shall go on dumbly feeling, though my martyrdom may last a million years!"

I made this appeal and held my peace. There was a full minute of unbroken silence and again another drop fell, but I knew with infinite unshakable certainty that everything would change immediately. And behold my grave suddenly was rent asunder, that is, I don't know whether it was opened or dug up, but I was caught up by some dark and unknown being and we found ourselves in space. I suddenly regained my sight. It was the dead of night, and never, never had there been such darkness. We were flying through space far away from the earth. I did not question the being who was taking me; I was proud and waited. I assured myself that I was not afraid, and was thrilled with ecstasy at the thought that I was not afraid. I do not know how long we were flying, I cannot imagine; it happened as it always does in dreams when you skip over space and time, and the laws of thought and existence, and only pause upon the points for which the heart yearns. I remember that I suddenly saw in the darkness a star. "Is that Sirius?" I asked impulsively, though I had not meant to ask questions.

"No, that is the star you saw between the clouds when you were coming home," the being who was carrying me replied.

I knew that it had something like a human face. Strange to say, I did not like that being, in fact I felt an intense aversion for it. I had expected complete non-existence, and that was why I had put a bullet through my heart. And here I was in the hands of a creature not human, of course, but yet living, existing. "And so there is life beyond the grave," I thought with the strange frivolity one has in dreams. But in its inmost depth my heart remained unchanged. "And if I have got to exist again," I thought, "and live once more under the control of some irresistible power, I won't be vanquished and humiliated."

"You know that I am afraid of you and despise me for that," I said suddenly to my companion, unable to refrain from the humiliating question which implied a confession, and feeling my humiliation stab my heart as with a pin. He did not answer my question, but all at once I felt that he was not even despising me, but was laughing at me and had no compassion for me, and that our journey had an unknown and mysterious object that concerned me only. Fear was growing in my heart. Something was mutely and painfully communicated to me from my silent companion, and permeated my whole being. We were flying through dark, unknown space. I had for some time lost sight of the constellations familiar to my eyes. I knew that there were stars in the heavenly spaces the light of which took thousands or millions of years to reach the earth. Perhaps we were already flying through those spaces. I expected something with a terrible anguish that tortured my heart. And suddenly I was thrilled by a familiar feeling that stirred me to the depths: I suddenly caught sight of our sun! I knew that it could not be our sun, that gave life to our earth, and that we were an infinite distance from our sun, but for some reason I knew in my whole being that it was a sun exactly like ours, a duplicate of it. A sweet, thrilling feeling resounded with ecstasy in my heart: the kindred power of the same light which had given me light stirred an echo in my heart and awakened it, and I had a sensation of life, the old life of the past for the first time since I had been in the grave.

"But if that is the sun, if that is exactly the same as our sun," I cried, "where is the earth?"

And my companion pointed to a star twinkling in the distance with an emerald light. We were flying straight towards it.

"And are such repetitions possible in the universe? Can that be the law of Nature?... And if that is an earth there, can it be just the same earth as ours... just the same, as poor, as unhappy, but precious and beloved for ever, arousing in the most ungrateful of her children the same poignant love for her that we feel for our earth?" I cried out, shaken by irresistible, ecstatic love for the old familiar earth which I had left. The image of the poor child whom I had repulsed flashed through my mind.

"You shall see it all," answered my companion, and there was a note of sorrow in his voice.

But we were rapidly approaching the planet. It was growing before my eyes; I could already distinguish the ocean, the outline of Europe; and suddenly a feeling of a great and holy jealousy glowed in my heart.

"How can it be repeated and what for? I love and can love only that earth which I have left, stained with my blood, when, in my ingratitude, I quenched my life with a bullet in my heart. But I have never, never ceased to love that earth, and perhaps on the very night I parted from it I loved it more than ever. Is there suffering upon this new earth? On our earth we can only love with suffering and through suffering. We cannot love otherwise, and we know of no other sort of love. I want suffering in order to love. I long, I thirst, this very instant, to kiss with tears the earth that I have left, and I don't want, I won't accept life on any other!"

But my companion had already left me. I suddenly, quite without noticing how, found myself on this other earth, in the bright light of a sunny day, fair as paradise. I believe I was standing on one of the islands that make up on our globe the Greek archipelago, or on the coast of the mainland facing that archipelago. Oh, everything was exactly as it is with us, only everything seemed to have a festive radiance, the splendour of some great, holy triumph attained at last. The caressing sea, green as emerald, splashed softly upon the shore and kissed it with manifest, almost conscious love. The tall, lovely trees stood in all the glory of their blossom, and their innumerable leaves greeted me, I am certain, with their soft, caressing rustle and seemed to articulate words of love. The grass glowed with bright and fragrant flowers. Birds were flying in flocks in the air, and perched fearlessly on my shoulders and arms and joyfully struck me with their darling, fluttering wings. And at last I saw and knew the people of this happy land. That came to me of themselves, they surrounded me, kissed me. The children of the sun, the children of their sun—oh, how beautiful they were! Never had I seen on our own earth such beauty in mankind. Only perhaps in our children, in their earliest years, one might find, some remote faint reflection of this beauty. The eyes of these happy people shone with a clear brightness. Their faces were radiant with the light of reason and fullness of a serenity that comes of perfect understanding, but those faces were gay; in their words and voices there was a note of childlike joy. Oh, from the first moment, from the first glance at them, I understood it all! It was the earth untarnished by the Fall; on it lived people who had not sinned. They lived just in such a paradise as that in which, according to all the legends of mankind, our first parents lived before they sinned; the only difference was that all this earth was the same paradise. These people, laughing joyfully, thronged round me and caressed me; they took me home with them, and each of them tried to reassure me. Oh, they asked me no questions, but they seemed, I fancied, to know everything without asking, and they wanted to make haste to smoothe away the signs of suffering from my face.

CHAPTER - IV

And do you know what? Well, granted that it was only a dream, yet the sensation of the love of those innocent and beautiful people has remained with me for ever, and I feel as though their love is still flowing out to me from over there. I have seen them myself, have known them and been convinced; I loved them, I suffered for them afterwards. Oh, I understood at once even at the time that in many things I could not understand them at all; as an up-to-date Russian progressive and contemptible Petersburger, it struck me as inexplicable that, knowing so much, they had, for instance, no science like our. But I soon realised that their knowledge was gained and fostered by intuitions different from those of us on earth, and that their aspirations, too, were quite different. They desired nothing and were at peace; they did not aspire to knowledge of life as we aspire to understand it, because their lives were full. But their knowledge was higher and deeper than ours; for our science seeks to explain what life is, aspires to understand it in order to teach others how to love, while they without science knew how to live; and that I understood, but I could not understand their knowledge. They showed me their trees, and I could not understand the intense love with which they looked at them; it was as though they were talking with creatures like themselves. And perhaps I shall not be mistaken if I say that they conversed with them. Yes, they had found their language, and I am convinced that the trees understood them. They looked at all Nature like that—at the animals who lived in peace with them and did not attack them, but loved them, conquered by their love. They pointed to the stars and told me something about them which I could not understand, but I am convinced that they were somehow in touch with the stars, not only in thought, but by some living channel. Oh, these people did not persist in trying to make me understand them, they loved me without that, but I knew that they would never understand me, and so I hardly spoke to them about our earth. I only kissed in their presence the earth on which they lived and mutely worshipped them themselves. And they saw that and let me worship them without being abashed at my adoration, for they themselves loved much. They were not unhappy on my account when at times I kissed their feet with tears, joyfully conscious of the love with which they would respond to mine. At times I asked myself with wonder how it was they were able never to offend a creature like me, and never once to arouse a feeling of jealousy or envy in me? Often I wondered how it could be that, boastful and untruthful as I was, I never talked to them of what I knew—of which, of course, they had no notion—that I was never tempted to do so by a desire to astonish or even to benefit them.

They were as gay and sportive as children. They wandered about their lovely woods and copses, they sang their lovely songs; their fair was light—the fruits of their trees, the honey from their woods, and the milk of the animals who loved them. The work they did for food and raiment was brief and not labourious. They loved and begot children, but I never noticed in them the impulse of that cruel sensuality which overcomes almost every man on this earth, all and each, and is the source of almost every sin of mankind on earth. They rejoiced at the arrival of children as new beings to share their happiness. There was no quarrelling, no jealousy among them, and they did not even know what the words meant. Their children were the children of all, for they all made up one family. There was scarcely any illness among them, though there was death; but their old people died peacefully, as though falling asleep, giving blessings and smiles to those who surrounded them to take their last farewell with bright and lovely smiles. I never saw grief or tears on those occasions, but only love, which reached the point of ecstasy, but a calm ecstasy, made perfect and contemplative. One might think that they were still in contact with the departed after death, and that their earthly union was not cut short by death. They scarcely understood me when I questioned them about immortality, but evidently they were so convinced of it without reasoning that it was not for them a question at all. They had no temples, but they had a real living and uninterrupted sense of oneness with the whole of the universe; they had no creed, but they had a certain knowledge that when their earthly joy had reached the limits of earthly nature, then there would come for them, for the living and for the dead, a still greater fullness of contact with the whole of the universe. They looked forward to that moment with joy, but without haste, not pining for it, but seeming to have a foretaste of it in their hearts, of which they talked to one another.

In the evening before going to sleep they liked singing in musical and harmonious chorus. In those songs they expressed all the sensations that the parting day had given them, sang its glories and took leave of it. They sang the praises of nature, of the sea, of the woods. They liked making songs about one another, and praised each other like children; they were the simplest songs, but they sprang from their hearts and went to one's heart. And not only in their songs but in all their lives they seemed to do nothing but admire one another. It was like being in love with each other, but an all-embracing, universal feeling.

Some of their songs, solemn and rapturous, I scarcely understood at all. Though I understood the words I could never fathom their full significance. It remained, as it were, beyond the grasp of my mind, yet my heart unconsciously absorbed it more and more. I often told them that I had had a presentiment of it long before, that this joy and glory had come to me on our earth in the form of a yearning melancholy that at times approached insufferable sorrow; that I had had a foreknowledge of them all and of their glory in the dreams of my heart and the visions of my mind; that often on our earth I could not look at the setting sun without tears... that in my hatred for the men of our earth there was always a yearning anguish: why could I not hate them without loving them? why could I not help forgiving them? and in my love for them there was a yearning grief: why could I not love them without hating them? They listened to me, and I saw they could not conceive what I was saying, but I did not regret that I had spoken to them of it: I knew that they understood the intensity of my yearning anguish over those whom I had left. But when they looked at me with their sweet eyes full of love, when I felt that in their presence my heart, too, became as innocent and just as theirs, the feeling of the fullness of life took my breath away, and I worshipped them in silence.

Oh, everyone laughs in my face now, and assures me that one cannot dream of such details as I am telling now, that I only dreamed or felt one sensation that arose in my heart in delirium and made up the details myself when I woke up. And when I told them that perhaps it really was so, my God, how they shouted with laughter in my face, and what mirth I caused! Oh, yes, of course I was overcome by the mere sensation of my dream, and that was all that was preserved in my cruelly wounded heart; but the actual forms and images of my dream, that is, the very ones I really saw at the very time of my dream, were filled with such harmony, were so lovely and enchanting and were so actual, that on awakening I was, of course, incapable of clothing them in our poor language, so that they were bound to become blurred in my mind; and so perhaps I really was forced afterwards to make up the details, and so of course to distort them in my passionate desire to convey some at least of them as quickly as I could. But on the other hand, how can I help believing that it was all true? It was perhaps a thousand times brighter, happier and more joyful than I describe it. Granted that I dreamed it, yet it must have been real. You know, I will tell you a secret: perhaps it was not a dream at all! For then something happened so awful, something so horribly true, that it could not have been imagined in a dream. My heart may have originated the dream, but would my heart alone have been capable of originating the awful event which happened to me afterwards? How could I alone have invented it or imagined it in my dream? Could my petty heart and fickle, trivial mind have risen to such a revelation of truth? Oh, judge for yourselves: hitherto I have concealed it, but now I will tell the truth. The fact is that I . . . corrupted them all!

CHAPTER - V

Yes, yes, it ended in my corrupting them all! How it could come to pass I do not know, but I remember it clearly. The dream embraced thousands of years and left in me only a sense of the whole. I only know that I was the cause of their sin and downfall. Like a vile trichina, like a germ of the plague infecting whole kingdoms, so I contaminated all this earth, so happy and sinless before my coming. They learnt to lie, grew fond of lying, and discovered the charm of falsehood. Oh, at first perhaps it began innocently, with a jest, coquetry, with amorous play, perhaps indeed with a germ, but that germ of falsity made its way into their hearts and pleased them. Then sensuality was soon begotten, sensuality begot jealousy, jealousy—cruelty . . . Oh, I don't know, I don't remember; but soon, very soon the first blood was shed. They marvelled and were horrified, and began to be split up and divided. They formed into unions, but it was against one another. Reproaches, upbraidings followed. They came to know shame, and shame brought them to virtue. The conception of honour sprang up, and every union began waving its flags. They began torturing animals, and the animals withdrew from them into the forests and became hostile to them. They began to struggle for separation, for isolation, for individuality, for mine and thine. They began to talk in different languages. They became acquainted with sorrow and loved sorrow; they thirsted for suffering, and said that truth could only be attained through suffering. Then science appeared. As they became wicked they began talking of brotherhood and humanitarianism, and understood those ideas. As they became criminal, they invented justice and drew up whole legal codes in order to observe it, and to ensure their being kept, set up a guillotine. They hardly remembered what they had lost, in fact, refused to believe that they had ever been happy and innocent. They even laughed at the possibility of this happiness in the past, and called it a dream. They could not even imagine it in definite form and shape, but, strange and wonderful to relate, though they lost all faith in their past happiness and called it a legend, they so longed to be happy and innocent once more that they succumbed to this desire like children, made an idol of it, set up temples and worshipped their own idea, their own desire; though at the same time they fully believed that it was unattainable and could not be realised, yet they bowed down to it and adored it with tears! Nevertheless, if it could have happened that they had returned to the innocent and happy condition which they had lost, and if someone had shown it to them again and had asked them whether they wanted to go back to it, they would certainly have refused. They answered me:

"We may be deceitful, wicked and unjust, we know it and weep over it, we grieve over it; we torment and punish ourselves more perhaps than that merciful Judge Who will judge us and whose Name we know not. But we have science, and by the means of it we shall find the truth and we shall arrive at it consciously. Knowledge is higher than feeling, the consciousness of life is higher than life. Science will give us wisdom, wisdom will reveal the laws, and the knowledge of the laws of happiness is higher than happiness."

That is what they said, and after saying such things everyone began to love himself better than anyone else, and indeed they could not do otherwise. All became so jealous of the rights of their own personality that they did their very utmost to curtail and destroy them in others, and made that the chief thing in their lives. Slavery followed, even voluntary slavery; the weak eagerly submitted to the strong, on condition that the latter aided them to subdue the still weaker. Then there were saints who came to these people, weeping, and talked to them of their pride, of their loss of harmony and due proportion, of their loss of shame. They were laughed at or pelted with stones. Holy blood was shed on the threshold of the temples. Then there arose men who began to think how to bring all people together again, so that everybody, while still loving himself best of all, might not interfere with others, and all might live together in something like a harmonious society. Regular wars sprang up over this idea. All the combatants at the same time firmly believed that science, wisdom and the instinct of self-preservation would force men at last to unite into a harmonious and rational society; and so, meanwhile, to hasten matters, 'the wise' endeavoured to exterminate as rapidly as possible all who were 'not wise' and did not understand their idea, that the latter might not hinder its triumph. But the instinct of self-preservation grew rapidly weaker; there arose men, haughty and sensual, who demanded all or nothing. In order to obtain everything they resorted to crime, and if they did not succeed—to suicide. There arose religions with a cult of non-existence and self-destruction for the sake of the everlasting peace of annihilation. At last these people grew weary of their meaningless toil, and signs of suffering came into their faces, and then they proclaimed that suffering was a beauty, for in suffering alone was there meaning. They glorified suffering in their songs. I moved about among them, wringing my hands and weeping over them, but I loved them perhaps more than in old days when there was no suffering in their faces and when they were innocent and so lovely. I loved the earth they had polluted even more than when it had been a paradise, if only because sorrow had come to it. Alas! I always loved sorrow and tribulation, but only for myself, for myself; but I wept over them, pitying them. I stretched out my hands to them in despair, blaming, cursing and despising myself. I told them that all this was my doing, mine alone; that it was I had brought them corruption, contamination and falsity. I besought them to crucify me, I taught them how to make a cross. I could not kill myself, I had not the strength, but I wanted to suffer at their hands. I yearned for suffering, I longed that my blood should be drained to the last drop in these agonies. But they only laughed at me, and began at last to look upon me as crazy. They justified me, they declared that they had only got what they wanted themselves, and that all that now was could not have been otherwise. At last they declared to me that I was becoming dangerous and that they should lock me up in a madhouse if I did not hold my tongue. Then such grief took possession of my soul that my heart was wrung, and I felt as though I were dying; and then . . . then I awoke.

It was morning, that is, it was not yet daylight, but about six o'clock. I woke up in the same arm-chair; my candle had burnt out; everyone was asleep in the captain's room, and there was a stillness all round, rare in our flat. First of all I leapt up in great amazement: nothing like this had ever happened to me before, not even in the most trivial detail; I had never, for instance, fallen asleep like this in my arm-chair. While I was standing and coming to myself I suddenly caught sight of my revolver lying loaded, ready - but instantly I thrust it away! Oh, now, life, life! I lifted up my hands and called upon eternal truth, not with words, but with tears; ecstasy, immeasurable ecstasy flooded my soul. Yes, life and spreading the good tidings! Oh, I at that moment resolved to spread the tidings, and resolved it, of course, for my whole life. I go to spread the tidings, I want to spread the tidings—of what? Of the truth, for I have seen it, have seen it with my own eyes, have seen it in all its glory.

And since then I have been preaching! Moreover I love all those who laugh at me more than any of the rest. Why that is so I do not know and cannot explain, but so be it. I am told that I am vague and confused, and if I am vague and confused now, what shall I be later on? It is true indeed: I am vague and confused, and perhaps as time goes on I shall be more so. And of course I shall make many blunders before I find out how to preach, that is, find out what words to say, what things to do, for it is a very difficult task. I see all that as clear as daylight, but, listen, who does not make mistakes? An yet, you know, all are making for the same goal, all are striving in the same direction anyway, from the sage to the lowest robber, only by different roads. It is an old truth, but this is what is new: I cannot go far wrong. For I have seen the truth; I have seen and I know that people can be beautiful and happy without losing the power of living on earth. I will not and cannot believe that evil is the normal condition of mankind. And it is just this faith of mine that they laugh at. But how can I help believing it? I have seen the truth—it is not as though I had invented it with my mind, I have seen it, seen it, and the living image of it has filled my soul for ever. I have seen it in such full perfection that I cannot believe that it is impossible for people to have it. And so how can I go wrong? I shall make some slips no doubt, and shall perhaps talk in second-hand language, but not for long: the living image of what I saw will always be with me and will always correct and guide me. Oh, I am full of courage and freshness, and I will go on and on if it were for a thousand years! Do you know, at first I meant to conceal the fact that I corrupted them, but that was a mistake—that was my first mistake! But truth whispered to me that I was lying, and preserved me and corrected me. But how establish paradise—I don't know, because I do not know how to put it into words. After my dream I lost command of words. All the chief words, anyway, the most necessary ones. But never mind, I shall go and I shall keep talking, I won't leave off, for anyway I have seen it with my own eyes, though I cannot describe what I saw. But the scoffers do not understand that. It was a dream, they say, delirium, hallucination. Oh! As though that meant so much! And they are so proud! A dream! What is a dream? And is not our life a dream? I will say more. Suppose that this paradise will never come to pass (that I understand), yet I shall go on preaching it. And yet how simple it is: in one day, in one hour everything could be arranged at once! The chief thing is to love others like yourself, that's the chief thing, and that's everything; nothing else is wanted—you will find out at once how to arrange it all. And yet it's an old truth which has been told and retold a billion times— but it has not formed part of our lives! The consciousness of life is higher than life, the knowledge of the laws of happiness is higher than happiness—that is what one must contend against. And I shall. If only everyone wants it, it can be arranged at once.

And I tracked down that little girl . . . and I shall go on and on!